Cheat!

Written by Judy Waite

Illustrated by Beryl Sanders

Daniel James Stokes
33 Chestnut Way
Woodend
Warwickshire
WO17 8BD

Chapter 1

It was Monday morning when the terrible thing happened.

Danny had just come down from getting dressed for school. He was wondering if Mum would notice that he hadn't done his tie up properly. In fact, he hadn't done his tie up at all; he'd just sort of twisted it round itself. He would take it off and push it into his pocket as soon as he got out the house.

He didn't even glance round at the sound of the postman. Mum stooped to pick up all the envelopes that dropped to the floor.

'Oh look, Danny, there's one
for you.'

Danny frowned. He never got
letters. It looked important too. It
was a long brown envelope. His full
name, '*Daniel James Stokes*', was typed
neatly on the outside. Puzzled, he
tore it open, unfolded the crisp white
letter and began to read:

Blackport Arts Council
18 Lower Quay Road
Blackport
Wales
BP6 7WG

16 September

Dear Daniel,

Following your entry to the Blackport Arts Council 'YOUNG ARTISTS' competition, we are delighted to tell you that you have won FIRST PRIZE.

We would like to invite you to a grand presentation on:
    Saturday October 12th, 2.30pm,
    Blackport Town Hall,
where you will receive a prize of £50 from the Lord Mayor.

Congratulations! We look forward to seeing you.

Yours sincerely,

A.C.Watson

A C Watson (Organiser)

Danny felt a sick, twisted feeling in his tummy. He closed his eyes, took a deep breath and counted to ten. It was something he had done ever since he was little, if horrible things happened. When he opened his eyes again, the horrible thing would be finished. It had worked on injections and nasty tasting medicine. It had worked on plasters that had to be pulled off quickly. It didn't work today. When he opened his eyes, the letter was still there.

He struggled to cram it back into its envelope, trying to hide it from Mum. It was no good. Mum was already beaming down on him.

'What is it Danny? It looks interesting.'

Danny handed it to her. As she read it, Mum shone with excitement.

'We must ring Gran. It was the competition you entered when you stayed with her. She'll want to see you get your prize. The town hall's not far from her house. I'm so proud of you, and to think Gran was worried about the way you're turning out.'

As Mum rattled on and on, Danny's head was spinning. What could he do? What could he say? He'd never thought in a million years that he'd win. He'd only entered to make Gran happy.

It was really hard to please his gran. She always made him feel clumsy and silly, as if he wasn't quite good enough. Then, when he was staying with her, he had done something terrible. He had stolen someone else's painting, and then pretended it was his.

He suddenly felt sick. What if the newspaper people were there? What if he was on television? Suppose Miss Baxter from school saw it? Even if Mum and Gran believed it, Miss Baxter would know he could *never* do a painting like that.

'You are pleased, aren't you?' Mum asked. 'You don't look very happy.'

Danny shrugged, trying to sound as if he wasn't really bothered. 'A bit shocked, that's all.'

He looked at the clock and pretended to jump in surprise, 'I've got to go. I said I'd meet Peter early. We've got a conker tournament before school starts.'

Shoving the letter into his rucksack, he turned and slammed out the door. He ignored Mum, calling behind him, 'Danny, don't crush that up. You ought to keep it safe somewhere. And you can't go yet – your tie's not done up properly...'

Why do you think Danny is feeling guilty?

Chapter 2

It had all started when Gran got him the art set.

Danny hated art. It was his worst subject at school. The only good thing about art was being able to flick paint at Jessica Jones when Miss Baxter wasn't looking.

He'd been staying with Gran for a week in the summer, and she said he was spending too much time 'hanging about'. She thought a boy his age should be 'developing his mind'. One day, as part of a trip into town, she'd dragged him into the art shop and bought him a set of paints and brushes.

Back home, she'd gone into the garden with a little table, plenty of clean water, and a mixing tray. Danny watched her fuss about, getting everything perfect. He had a heavy, sinking feeling. He was bound to disappoint her in the end. Mum always said he shouldn't take any notice of Gran's grumbling. She said it was just her 'way'. Sometimes, though, Danny got the feeling that Mum was a bit scared of Gran too.

Once Gran had left, Danny spent an interesting five minutes blobbing different colours onto the paper. He'd watched them spread, then run together. Then he got bored. He wandered down to the furthest end of the garden. He could poke around in the dead leaves. Maybe he would find some snails or worms to paint.

It was then that he saw the hole in the fence. It was quite a big hole – boy-sized, in fact. Danny was sure it wouldn't hurt to have a quick peep.

He could do a bit of exploring. He might even discover something worth painting. He glanced behind to make sure Gran was still safely indoors, then wriggled through.

It was more like a jungle than a garden. Everything was wild and overgrown. The grass grew as high as his chin. In one corner, almost hidden by ivy, was an ancient tumbledown shed.

Danny knew whose garden it was. It belonged to old Mr King. He was Gran's blind neighbour. Danny had never actually met him, but Gran was always going round there with meat pies. She spent ages baking them, grumbling that the old man wasn't eating properly. Danny had never gone next door with her. The idea of Mr King being blind frightened him. He'd never seen a blind person. He wasn't sure how you looked at them, or what you said.

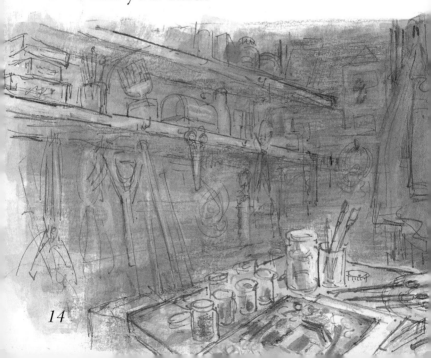

Danny felt quite safe as he looked around the garden. Everything was so overgrown, Mr King couldn't have been in it for years.

Feeling like a real adventurer Danny crept towards the shed. The door was half open and it creaked as he pushed against it. Inside the shed it was dark and musty. The window had ivy growing across it. Danny stood for a moment while his eyes got used to the gloom.

There were shapes and shadows. There were old tins and tools. Everything was covered with thick cobwebs. There was ivy inside the shed too. It had crept in through the gaps in the wood. For a moment it startled Danny, brushing against his bare arm.

In the corner something moved – rustled. Danny stiffened. Perhaps it was a mouse – or a rat. Perhaps this wasn't such a good idea after all.

Suddenly something was standing, looming over him; something tall and shadowy. Danny tried to swing round. In his panic, he knocked his elbow against the wall. There was the crash of things falling. Then, as the clatter and rattle died away, Danny heard breathing. It was a harsh, rasping sound. Through the gloom, a long, bony hand reached towards him …

Chapter 3

'Who's that? Who is it?' The voice was old, cracked.

'Danny…Danny Stokes. From next door.'

Danny shook as he spoke. His eyes were screwed tight shut. He wanted to run but he was too scared. He was frozen to the spot.

'Just a boy, a child.' The voice, speaking to itself, seemed to relax. 'You didn't smell like anyone dangerous. Are you Dora's grandson?'

Danny wasn't sure he liked the idea of being *smelt* but he nodded.

'Yes.'

He looked up, and saw the grey, sightless eyes of Mr King turned towards him.

'You startled me. I didn't hear you coming. Usually I hear everything.' Mr King moved backwards slowly, groping the air.

Danny watched him as he struggled and fumbled. He felt ashamed. The old man must have been much more scared than he was. At least Danny could *see* what was going on.

Danny suddenly noticed the jutting legs of a fallen table. He saw a broken jar and some paint brushes. They were scattered across the shed floor. 'Be careful, Mr King. There's glass on the floor, and your table got knocked over.' He grabbed one end of the table and began to lift. He was glad of the chance to do something useful.

Mr King grasped the edge of it. 'There's a broom in the corner.

Could you sweep up the mess, lad? I'll only make things worse if I try.'

As he bent down, Danny noticed a large sheet of paper. It would be perfect to put the glass in. He reached for it, then sat, stunned. It was a half-finished painting of a garden. The trees were heavy with blossom. Everywhere there were flowers. In the corner, beautifully twined with clambering roses, was a wooden shed. It wasn't perfect. There was a childlike feel about it. The colours were too bright. The flowers were too big. The shed had funny angles. Somehow, though, it all added together to make it even more interesting.

Danny looked up at Mr King. 'This is a brilliant painting. Did you do it?'

The old man smiled and the smile shone in his eyes. Danny realised there was nothing scary about looking at him at all.

'From memory. I don't suppose it still looks like this now. But it did once, when I was a lad.' Mr King turned his face to the window. He couldn't see the dust, or the cobwebs, or the tangle of ivy. He could only see the beautiful garden that lived in his imagination.

Danny whistled. 'It's miles better than anything I could have done. Shall I put it on the table for you?'

Mr King shook his head, 'It's ruined for me now. I can't ever stop you see. Not 'til I've finished. I don't know what bit I've got to. I'll start a new one tomorrow.'

'I'm sorry.' Danny felt terrible. Because of him, Mr King couldn't finish his wonderful painting.

'Not to worry lad. It was nice to have a visitor. I don't get a lot of excitement,' Mr King chuckled, then added, 'although perhaps you'd better let me know you're coming next time.'

Danny was about to ask if he could visit the next time Gran made a meat pie, when he heard a sharp call. 'Help, that's Gran. I shouldn't be here. She'll kill me if she finds out where I've been.'

Mr King chuckled again, 'I won't tell, if you don't.'

'Thanks.'

23

Danny hurried away from the shed. He wriggled through the hole in the fence. He ran back to the table and the pots of paints in Gran's garden. It was only then that he realised he was still holding Mr King's painting.

He could hear the heavy tread of Gran's shoes as she grew nearer. He frowned at the splodges he had painted earlier. They looked stupid, childish. Gran would be cross with him for not trying hard enough. Danny made a sudden decision.

Snatching the paper, he crumpled it up and threw it into the bushes. Then he hurriedly smoothed Mr King's painting out on to the table. As Gran appeared, he began mixing the green for the clump of bushes he had decided to add in one corner of the painting.

What do you think is Danny's 'sudden decision'?

Chapter 4

He hadn't felt guilty – not even the next day, when Gran showed him the entry form in the local paper.

'I think we'll enter that painting of yours,' she said. She cut the form out and handed Danny a pen. 'You made such a good effort. It just shows how well you can do, when you try.'

Danny filled in his name – his age – his address. All the evidence, neatly written for the world to see.

That same afternoon he went round with Gran to deliver a meat pie to Mr King. It was funny, having to pretend they didn't know each other.

Mr King shook his hand and said he was 'delighted to have met him at last'. He even told Danny he could come over and play in his garden if he were ever bored.

Mr King's house felt warm and cheerful. Danny noticed he had pictures everywhere. They seemed bright and lively; not musty and dark, like the ones in the town museum where Gran sometimes dragged him. It seemed odd, though, having all these pictures and not being able to see them.

'Have you always been blind, Mr King?'

'*Danny!*' Gran's voice was shocked, but Mr King just smiled.

'Don't worry, Dora. He's just a lad.'

He turned to Danny. Even though his eyes weren't looking at him, Mr King still somehow seemed to see him.

'I was about your age. My eyesight was never good, but as I got older, it grew worse. Things got more and more blurry. And then, one day, I woke up and the world was completely black.'

'Weren't you scared?' It was so hard to imagine. Danny thought of all the things he would miss: football, telly, computer games. Poor Mr King. He could never be really free. Even his house was only safe as long as nothing got moved.

'I suppose I learnt to make the best of it. But it upset my father more than anything. He was an artist – a good one too. Most of these pictures were his. And he'd had hopes for me. I'd shown promise once…' The old man's voice trailed away, lost in distant memories.

Danny thought suddenly about the painting of the garden. He wished he could tell Mr King that he'd treasure it forever. Maybe he'd find a way to tell him later. He couldn't say anything with Gran there.

He turned to ask another question, but Gran stopped him. 'That's enough, Danny! We really must be going. You're off home later today, and you've got packing to do.'

She got up and Danny followed, looking back just once. Mr King was smiling after them; that kind, gentle smile that lit up the blankness in his eyes.

Even then, Danny still hadn't felt guilty. Not until now when he was going to be found out. He sat on his bed after school. The morning's letter lay like something poisonous beside him. Danny buried his face in his hands and wondered if that was the worst crime of all: not just telling lies to Gran; not just pretending he had done something when he hadn't; not even cheating on kind, gentle Mr King.

The worst crime of all was that he hadn't even felt guilty about it.

Chapter 5

It was the day of the presentation.

As Mum drove them to Blackport, Danny sat hunched in his seat. He kept hoping they would break down, or get stuck in an enormous traffic jam. Instead, the car zoomed along happily, and the road stayed clear.

They arrived with plenty of time to spare.

Danny saw the painting as soon as they walked into the town hall.

It was hanging at the front of the room. A tag with the words, *1ST PRIZE*, was on the wall next to the painting.

Mum tried to drag Danny towards it, but he pulled away. 'I've seen it before,' he muttered.

Mum squeezed his arm proudly. 'You shouldn't be so shy about it.'

Danny watched her hurry towards the painting. He wondered if there were still time to get out of the presentation. Perhaps he could pretend to faint. Perhaps he could say he felt sick.

He decided the 'being sick' idea would work best.

Mum came back, buzzing with excitement. 'It's brilliant. I never knew you had such a wonderful talent.'

Danny gave a groan of pain, and clutched his stomach. 'I don't feel very well.'

'I'm sure it's just nerves. You'll be fine once it all gets started.' Mum glanced up at the hall clock. 'We'd better go and sit down. The Mayor will be here soon.'

Danny trudged behind her. They squeezed in amongst the rows of chairs that were already filling up with people. He couldn't even try out the 'fainting' plan. There wasn't enough room to fall over properly.

Mum nudged him suddenly, 'Look, Gran's here.'

Danny turned miserably towards the door. Gran was walking in, her arm linked with someone else. Danny hadn't known it was possible to feel any worse, but the 'rock' in his stomach hit a new low. The smiling, shuffling figure coming in with Gran was Mr King.

The buzz of voices died. The Mayor of Blackport strode importantly to the front and cleared his throat.

Danny didn't hear the speech. The presentations to the runner-up prize winners passed over him like a blur.

'And now, could we have our Young Artist of the Year – Danny Stokes …' The Mayor's voice seemed to boom and bounce through the hall.

Danny got up and walked towards the front. He couldn't look at Mum. He couldn't look at Gran. He couldn't go through with it. Danny closed his eyes, and counted to ten. As he opened them slowly, he looked straight across at Mr King.

Although Mr King couldn't see, his eyes still shone with warmth and pride.

'Congratulations,' the Mayor said, smiling and shaking Danny's hand. 'It's a wonderful entry, a very worthy winner.'

Danny took the envelope. It felt bulky and exciting. He imagined the notes inside. Fifty pounds – it was loads of money. It could buy him a new computer game or maybe a football shirt, but he knew, deep down, that he'd never really enjoy them. They would never *really* be his.

He turned to face the audience. His voice was small, croaky.

'I'm really pleased I won this. And ... and I want to spend it on something really special.'

As he paused, he felt a rush of feelings flood through him. He knew with certainty that he was doing the right thing. Suddenly his voice became clear and strong.

'I've decided to give it to the Blind Association. I reckon they might need it more than I need a new computer game.'

For a moment there was a stunned silence. Then all at once the clapping started. The Mayor was squeezing his shoulder. People were rising to their feet. Through the swell of faces Danny could see Mum, dabbing at her eyes with a hanky.

Everyone was cheering as he battled his way to his seat. Strangers reached out to shake his hand or pat his back. Warm voices called out praises and congratulations. He was everybody's favourite. He was everybody's hero.

Mum hugged him tightly and Gran *almost* kissed him – although he managed to turn his head away just in time. It ended up as just a bit of slobber on his ear.

But the thing that really did it, the thing that made his heart do another crash landing, was Mr King. The old man rose to his feet, stretching his fingertips to touch Danny's face. His eyes shone like lights.

'Not many lads would do that,' he said. 'You're even better than I first thought. You're something special, Danny. You're a really good lad.'

Danny stood, staring dumbly back

at Mr King. It was all going wrong
again – horribly wrong.

Danny didn't feel 'good' at all.

How did Danny try to put things right?

How has it all gone wrong again?

Chapter 6

Back at her house, Gran had prepared a party.

She'd baked a huge cake in the shape of an artist's palette. Across the top she'd iced the words '*Well Done Danny*'. She'd made biscuits and sandwiches in strange shapes and colours. She even gave Danny a present. It was a glossy, new book called '*Let's Look at Painting*'.

Danny flicked through the pages, and munched miserably on a cucumber sandwich. The only good thing was that Mr King had turned down Gran's invitation to join them.

He said he'd 'already had enough excitement for one day'. If he'd been there, he might have wanted to talk about art, and brush sizes, or whatever it was that real artists talked about.

Danny realised, sadly, that he might never be able to face seeing Mr King again.

Gran insisted he had a giant wedge of the 'paint palette'. The sight of it made Danny feel really sick. He decided to wedge the cake in the side of his mouth, like a hamster. He could feed it to Gran's rubber plant when no one was looking. The shrill ring of the doorbell saved him from being forced to eat a bright green biscuit in the shape of a paint brush.

As Gran bustled out to answer the door, Mum leaned across and rumpled Danny's hair.

'I think you've really proved something to Gran today. I don't think she'll ever grumble about you again.'

Before Danny had time to grunt his reply, Gran reappeared. She was smiling, almost girlishly, up at a man with a pony tail and an earring. Danny nearly choked on the piece of cake, which had escaped from its hiding place in his cheek. Gran usually tutted and grumbled about men with pony tails and earrings. Now, here she was, happily inviting one into her house!

The man strode across the room, 'Hi there. I'm Ricky Thomson, a reporter from *Blackport News*.'

Gran offered him a chair and he pulled it up close to Danny.

'It's great to meet you, Danny. I've heard all about you – a real Super Hero! I just want a quick chat. Maybe take a few pictures.' Already his notebook was out, open on a blank page. 'It's a great painting. Tell me, how long did it take you to do?'

'I...'

'Not long,' Gran said as she plonked an enormous chunk of the 'paint palette' in front of the reporter. 'He just sat out in the garden one day in the holidays and got on with it. He's not one to mess about, not our Danny.'

'Great.' The reporter was writing furiously, 'And how long have you been painting for?'

'I...'

'Not long. That's the amazing thing,' Gran rattled on. 'He's never really bothered before. He must be a true genius to come up with that without proper training.' She pointed

44

to the painting. It was now hanging on a hook which had, until yesterday, held a faded portrait of Gran as a child.

'That's really great! And what do your school mates think about it all?'

'I...' Danny shot a desperate glance at Mum, but she was gazing at him with a mushy, glowing sort of expression as if she'd just seen a choir of heavenly angels float down from the ceiling. 'I... I haven't told them.'

'See,' said Gran cutting more cake for the reporter, 'modest, as well as talented and generous.'

'Great!' Ricky Thompson shut the notebook. He flashed a dazzling smile, and pulled a camera out of his bag. 'Now, how about those pictures. That's one sure way we can let your mates know what a Wonder Kid you are.'

To Danny it seemed as if the room were growing smaller and smaller, pressing into him, trapping him. He had to get away.

'I...I won't be long. I need the loo.'

He walked as steadily as he could, out into the hall. His trainers were beside the door. It didn't take a minute to put them on.

In the background he could still hear Gran rattling away. 'Oh yes. *Ever* such a good boy. We're all *so* proud of him.'

He opened the front door as quietly as he could. With luck, it would be at least five minutes before anyone realised he'd gone.

Chapter 7

He bumped into the woman as he rushed out through the gate.

She was dressed in a violent pink suit, wearing lots of make-up. Her frizzy hair looked as if it had been dried while she was upside down.

Danny went to dodge round her. Suddenly he became aware of a small crowd of people gathered on the pavement. There was a posh car parked nearby. Two men with headphones on were pulling wires out of the back of a van.

'Danny Stokes?' The frizzy-haired woman was smiling at him.

Danny noticed she had pink lipstick stains on her teeth.

'I...'

She held out her hand and flashed her teeth again. 'I'm Jenni Lake, *Network Television News*. These are my crew.' She waved her arm across at the men who were walking towards them carrying giant cameras.

'We were hoping you could spare us a few minutes for an interview. Everyone is *so* impressed by what you've done.'

The crowd was getting bigger. People were pushing and jostling for a better view. Danny wondered if he could pretend he'd never even heard of anyone called 'Danny Stokes'. Then a murmur from the crowd made him look round.

Mr King was coming out of his house. Someone was walking beside him. Someone else was doing a backwards run, pointing a camera at Mr King's face. Jenni Lake was talking again.

'We wanted to get you both together. Telling us about how you met and why you decided to donate your prize money like that. It's such a *lovely* story.'

From the corner of his eye Danny saw Gran's front door open. Ricky Thomson sprang out, followed closely by Gran and Mum. Gran was carrying the painting.

This was it. There was no escape. He would have to go on T.V. with Mr King. Everyone in the whole world would think he was a brilliant painter. He would have to keep cheating and lying for the rest of his life.

Jenni Lake was a quick worker. Within minutes she had the cameras set up in Gran's front garden. She began flashing her smile into one of the cameras. 'This seems like an ordinary house, in an ordinary street, but the young person we have come to talk to is no ordinary boy.'

The camera swung round to the gate where Danny now stood, beside Mr King. The painting was propped up between them.

'Danny, could you tell us a little bit about the picture? It really is quite *lovely*.'

Danny closed his eyes. He tried counting to ten, but he couldn't concentrate. He knew there was only one thing to do.

Swallowing hard, he looked straight at the camera. He felt hot, then cold, then shaky. But when he spoke, his voice was louder than he'd expected. It was angry, almost shouting.

'I'm not who you all think I am. I'm the worst person in the world.'

'Now Danny...' Jenni Lake gave a nervous laugh. Danny ignored her.

He was going to get this over with. Nothing would stop him now.

'I'm not the wonderful hero you all keep saying I am. The person you should really be amazed by is this man here, Mr King. *He* did the painting. I stole it from him.'

The crowd shifted uneasily. Jenni Lake's violent pink lips dropped open in horror. The silence was enormous.

Danny couldn't stand it any longer. He'd said what he had to say, now he just wanted to get away from everybody.

Before anyone could stop him, Danny suddenly leapt over the fence and hurtled down the road like a rocket.

How do you think Danny feels now that he has owned up?

Chapter 8

He wanted to run for ever. He
wanted *never* to go home and face
Mum, or Gran, or Mr King. It
seemed like a long time before he let
himself slow to a walk. He didn't
know where he was or where he'd
been. It didn't matter. He just had to
keep moving.

It was getting late. The street
lamps came on. Lights, warm and
friendly, lit up the front rooms of the
houses that he passed. His tummy
rumbled, telling him it was way past
supper time. He even found himself
thinking longingly about the 'paint

palette' cake. Danny supposed he'd have to stop soon, and try and find somewhere to sleep. It was then that he realised, with a cold horror, where he was.

It was Gran's road; the end he didn't usually come down. He must have been walking in a kind of loop. His first thought was to run again. Then suddenly he realised that it didn't matter. However fast he ran, and however far he went, he couldn't get away from himself. And it was himself he really couldn't stand to be with.

Slowly, he walked down the pavement towards Gran's house. The curtains were drawn and Mum's car was still in the drive. At least she hadn't gone home without him. He pictured them both, sitting together in Gran's front room. Gran would be grumbling at Mum. She'd be moaning about how awful Danny was. Mum would probably be agreeing.

As Danny reached the gate, he paused. He couldn't face them yet. He needed time to think. Time to work out the right thing to say. He pushed open the rusted little gate that led up to Mr King's house. Very quietly, he crept round to the back of the building.

It was completely dark. Another time, Danny would have been scared. Another time, the whispering, rustling garden would have seemed full of dangers.

Now, though, Danny was too tired to care. He pushed through the blackness, his hands feeling his way past the bushes and branches. At last he came to the shed.

The door creaked again as he stepped inside. It was too dark to see anything. Danny felt the edge of the table against his leg. He trod on something that clattered and rolled. Reaching out, he felt for the chair. Suddenly his hand touched something warm – something human.

'Danny, I was hoping you'd come.'
There was no surprise in Mr King's
voice. Danny guessed he had heard
him stumbling down the garden.
Probably smelt him as he came in.

He stood, awkward and ashamed.
What was the old man thinking? Why
didn't he shout at him? Why did he
have to be so *nice*?

'I suppose you hate me.'

'I don't hate you, Danny. What
you did today was brave – strong.
You could have just kept that prize.
You could have gone on the
television and taken all the praise.
No one would ever have known.'

Danny shook his head, 'I cheated.
And I lied.'

'You've done the hardest bit, telling the truth.'

'But Gran will...'

Mr King cut in. 'Your Gran can be a real dragon. I'm not surprised she terrifies you. She terrifies me sometimes too.' He paused. 'I'll tell you a little secret – something your Gran doesn't know – something I couldn't dare to tell her. I'm vegetarian.'

For a moment, Danny forgot his own problems. 'But all those meat pies; what do you do with them?'

Mr King chuckled, 'In the bin. As soon as she's gone. I've been doing that for years now. Just haven't got the guts to tell her.' He was silent for a moment and then added, 'And the thing you had to admit to was much, much worse.'

'I bet *she* hates me,' said Danny, 'and I bet she's been blaming Mum too.'

'They're both upset.' Mr King reached out and touched him in the darkness. 'They had a row. Your mum shouted and said your gran was always too hard on you. Then your gran shouted and said it was only because she wanted you to turn out well. It did them the world of good to let off steam with each other for once.'

'And what about the T.V. and the newspaper? Everyone will know.'

'They've both agreed not to run the story.'

Danny's eyes widened. 'But why?'

'I had a word with them. Mind you, they struck a hard bargain. Jenni Lake got me to agree to an interview for some series she's doing called, "Hidden Senses", and that reporter chap wants to run an article about how folk like me cope in my own home.'

'I'm sorry. I bet that meant even more problems for you.'

'Not a bit,' Mr King sounded
almost boyish. 'It livened me up. I'd
never expected so much excitement
at my time of life.'

Danny stood for a long time,
feeling suddenly very small.

'I suppose I'd better go and face
Mum and Gran. Get it over with.'

Mr King squeezed his shoulder. 'It may not be as bad as you think. But whatever happens, you owe it to them to explain what you did; not to run away from it. And they're both worried sick. Your gran was all for calling the police, but your mum was hoping you'd go back on your own.'

Danny bit his lip hard. 'Will you come with me?'

Mr King took him firmly by the elbow, 'Ready when you are.'

Slowly, they walked together, back through the tangled garden. They reached Gran's front door and Danny lifted the knocker. Mr King turned to him, 'And there's another thing you should know; something that might make you feel better.'

'What's that?' Danny's tummy was beginning to knot up. He couldn't imagine anything making him feel better.

Mr King pointed upwards,
towards the stars. 'If my old dad's up
there, looking down at me, I reckon
he'll be very proud.'
'Why?'

'Well I'm eighty one, and completely blind, but I still came first in a painting competition. Daft as it sounds, that really meant something to me.'

Danny looked up at the night that Mr King couldn't see. He looked at Mr King. He wondered how many years it took to get as wise, and as kind, as he was.

He turned back to the door. Through the dappled glass two figures appeared in the hall.

Danny closed his eyes, took a deep breath, and counted to ten.

What will Danny say to Mum and Gran?

Have you ever owned up to something you did wrong?